The Pirate, Big Fist, and Me

by M. J. Cosson

ILLUSTRATED BY BRANN GARVEY

Librarian Reviewer
Marci Peschke
Librarian, Dallas Independent School District
M.A. Education Reading Specialist, Stephen F. Austin State University
Learning Resources Endorsement, Texas Women's University

Reading Consultant
Mark DeYoung
Classroom Teacher, Edina Public Schools, MN
B.A. in Elementary Education, Central College
M.S. in Curriculum & Instruction, University of MN

STONE ARCH BOOKS
Minneapolis   San Diego

Vortex Books are published by Stone Arch Books,
151 Good Counsel Drive, P.O. Box 669,
Mankato, Minnesota 56002.
www.stonearchbooks.com

Library of Congress Cataloging-in-Publication Data
Cosson, M. J.

    The Pirate, Big Fist, and Me / by M. J. Cosson; illustrated by Brann
Garvey.

    p. cm. — (Vortex Bbooks)

    Summary: Levi Viggers the Eighth, descendent of a pirate, must serve
a year of after-school detention in the library where he comes across a book
that reveals some old family secrets, leading him to team up with his bullying
cousin in a search for buried treasure.

    ISBN-13: 978-1-59889-068-6 (hardcover)

    ISBN-10: 1-59889-068-9 (hardcover)

    ISBN-13: 978-1-59889-279-6 (paperback)

    ISBN-10: 1-59889-279-7 (paperback)

    [1. Buried treasure—Fiction. 2. Cousins—Fiction. 3. Pirates—Fiction.]
I. Garvey, Brann, ill. II. Title. III. Series.
PZ7.C8193Pi 2007
[Fic]—dc22
                          2006007681

Art Director: Heather Kindseth
Graphic Designer: Kay Fraser

Photo Credits
Corel, cover (snake tail)
Karon Dubke, cover (coins and notebook)
Shutterstock\Casey K, Bishop, cover (snake head)

1 2 3 4 5 6 11 10 09 08 07 06

Printed in the United States of America

Table of CONTENTS

Chapter 1

DOING TIME

I'm Levi Viggers the Eighth. No middle name. Just Levi Viggers. I'm the eighth person in my family with this name. You could say I'm like King Henry the Eighth. But I'm not a king. The first Levi Viggers was a pirate.

Being a pirate is bad. But being related to a pirate is not so bad. In fact, it can be very good. I used to think it meant I was bad. So did Big Fist.

But now I know what it really means.

It means I have a sense for adventure.

It means I'm daring.

It means I'm rich.

Well, the first two are true. The last point is still under debate.

I found out about the pirate in a strange way. A few months ago I got into trouble. It wasn't anything serious. I just didn't come straight home from school a few times. Dad was gone, and Mom freaked.

My grades weren't so great, either. So the adults in my life (except Dad) decided that I needed help. They said I needed to spend time at the library. This wasn't just a grounding for a week or two. It was for the whole school year. I had to show "marked improvement." My counselor said it was supposed to make a new person out of me. It did. It made a pirate out of me.

Every day I had to check in at the library by 3:45. I couldn't check out until 5:30. That way, Mom would be back from work when I got home. Mom told me to think of it as an extra study hall. I know she was worried about me because Dad was gone.

Basically, I was being babysat in the library by this retired volunteer, Mr. Zylstra. He was the one I checked in and out with. Other than that, we never talked. He mostly put books back on the shelves. He also gave me the evil eye if I was loud.

So I was doing time at the library. But that wasn't the worst part. I could live with the library. I even liked it. However, Big Fist, my least favorite person in the world, was doing library time too. He's my second or third cousin on Dad's side. His real name is Bill Viggers the Fifth. (We're big on names with numbers in my family.)

In first grade Bill proved he had the ability to punch people. Now everybody just calls him Big Fist. That's what you get if you look at him wrong, his big fist.

He's a big, beefy guy, and he has big, beefy fists. In the second, third, and fifth grades I had the pleasure of experiencing the big fist myself. Most kids around here have experienced it at one time or another.

People learn to avoid Big Fist.

That first day at the library, I saw Big Fist before he saw me. I figured I was safe inside the library, and it worked out that way.

Big Fist is smart enough to know that you don't pound people in the library. Outside the library, though, is a different matter. I was fair game.

I could tell Mom felt a little bad about me having to spend all that time in the library.

So she gave me Dad's e-mail address. She said I could use the library computer to e-mail him if I didn't have homework.

Dad's in Iraq for the third time. He's a Marine. I think Mom was worried that I wasn't getting enough manly advice at this stage of my life.

Anyway, when I first spotted Big Fist that first day, I knew he was doing library time too. Why else would he be hanging around the library? Big Fist wasn't really into books.

Just to be safe, I tried staying out of his way at the library. I always kept a few bookshelves between him and me. Then, one day, I ducked into a little room with the words "Local History" on the door. That's where I found the pirate.

THE ORIGINAL

I closed the door of the Local History room. It was dim inside, but there were reading lights. I decided it would make a great nap room. I was pretty sure it was empty most of the time. I'd never seen anybody in it. I sat down in a rocking chair and thought about what I could be doing if I had my freedom. I could be hanging out with friends. I could be playing video games. I could be zoning out in front of the TV at home.

I sat in the chair and stared at the shelves of books in the room. A shabby old book titled *Our Town's History* popped out at me. I don't know why I noticed it. I picked it up and began to read.

The book was really neat. It was written by hand more than a hundred years ago. Its pages were yellow and stained. Some of it was hard to read. The writer talked to old folks and wrote down their memories. Some people told stories about the **first** Levi Viggers. Turns out he was here way before this town was even built!

The people said that Levi the First had worked with the famous pirate Jean Lafitte. From 1817 to 1820, Lafitte was based on Galveston Island. That's just up the coast from our town. And before that he was in New Orleans. That's just up the coast from Galveston.

In 1820, the government kicked Lafitte and his men off Galveston Island. So Lafitte left the country. Probably some of his men went with him to Mexico. But the rest of them probably took their share of the loot and settled down. That's when Levi Viggers showed up.

The book said Levi became a farmer and fisherman. I didn't know there had been a farm in the family. This town is full of people named Viggers and people married to people named Viggers. In fact, about half this town seems to be family. There aren't any farms around here anymore, though. The soil isn't all that great for farming. There are mostly oil refineries and sand dunes.

The book also told about a rumor. The rumor was that the first Levi Viggers left a buried treasure. As of a hundred years ago, nobody had found the treasure.

That caught my attention! I wondered how I could find clues. That's when I remembered I had my dad's e-mail address.

I sent him this note:

Hey Dad,

How's Iraq? I hope you're keeping safe. I know Mom tells you everything when she e-mails every day. I won't bore you with details about my library time. It's okay, I guess. I'm fine with it. My grades will probably get better.

I have a question, though. I found a book here called Our Town's History. Have you ever heard of it? It says the first Levi Viggers was a pirate with Jean Lafitte. It says that he left a buried treasure. That is so cool. What do you know about it?

Your loving son, L

When I finished my email, I looked at the little clock on the computer. It was almost six. I'd been so wrapped up in the book and my e-mail to Dad, I lost track of time.

I didn't even have to worry about ducking out of the library or leaving with a crowd. Big Fist was long gone.

Chapter 3

The next day when I got to the library, I had a message from Dad. He wrote:

Hey Kid,

Things are quiet over here for the time being. But I'm counting the days until I can come home again.

I'm glad you're spending time at the library. It will be good for you. And now that you have a computer to use, we can keep in touch better.

I didn't know there was a book in the library about Levi the First. But do you remember the song about the treasure? I used to sing you to sleep with it when you were little. My dad sang it to me. It goes to the tune of "Yankee Doodle Dandy." I'll write it all out below. Hope I can remember all the words because they're supposed to be clues.

Maybe you'll remember it when you read it. The story goes that the song came from Levi the First, and he sang it to his son, Levi the Second. So it's come all the way down the generations. It's probably good that it's getting written down here so we can have a record of it. Some of the words might have been changed or lost over the years. It's called "The Treasure Song."

Jean Lafitte was a gentleman.

He gave his men fair share.

He split his treasure a thousand ways.

And faded into air.

I buried my taking in the dust

Near the mouth of Horseshoe Bay.

Its riches will bring health and happiness

To all who taste the way.

Listen as the wind blows free

And watch as the rocks crumble dry.

The treasure will grow, generations
  will see,

And pits will rise to the sky.

So shake my hand and twist just so,

Be mindful to scrape the rust.

Take care that the sun shines on it too,

So the gold doesn't turn to dust.

When I read the words, I remembered the song. I hummed to myself as I reread the clues. When I was little the words didn't mean anything. Nobody had told me that it was a family song. Or that it was a clue to pirate treasure. My first thought was that this was all a joke. I wrote to Dad and asked him if it was real.

I got this reply the next day.

L,

Welcome to the Viggers Rite of Passage. Every Levi Viggers comes to realize the words to the song might mean something. I remember when it hit me. I was about ten. I spent years looking for that treasure.

I'm still looking.

I don't think any Viggers has ever found out about Levi the First and Lafitte in a library book before. That's got to be a first!

Too bad Grandpa isn't still around. He would have loved to help you search.

Here's a clue if you want to search for the treasure. I remember looking in this place. I didn't find it, but you have to start somewhere. Go to the south end of the marsh, about a half mile north of the shrimpers' docks. If you follow the edge of the marsh, there's a dry creek. Follow the creek to a bend.

You'll find a shallow cave in the bend. The cave is rust colored, which is a clue in the song. Look in there, but watch out for rattlers and scorpions. In fact, watch out for snakes all along that creek bed!

Good luck,

Dad

I couldn't wait for 5:30. I was so excited I didn't even try to avoid Big Fist. He hadn't seemed to notice me anyway.

 21

The next day was Saturday. It was easy to find the cave. It was just like Dad had described it.

I threw a couple of rocks in to scare out any animals. Nothing came out.

The cave was pretty shallow. I could see to the back wall from outside.

I climbed in. The cave was big enough that I could stand up in it.

I looked carefully at the walls on both sides. Then I began to study the ceiling. Suddenly something shot toward me.

I yelled and jumped out of the cave. I landed on the creek bed about five feet below the cave. I twisted an ankle as I rolled onto the rocks. The thing scurried past me.

It was a big, fat lizard that had been taking a snooze out of the morning sun.

My heart was beating triple time. I sat on the rocks holding my sore ankle and watching the blood ooze from the scratches up and down my right arm. At least I'd worn jeans so my legs weren't all gashed up too.

I turned and looked at the cave. From where I sat, it looked like a big, laughing mouth. I wondered again if Dad was pulling tricks on me. The Viggers's humor is kind of like that. Relatives are always playing tricks on each other.

When my foot quit throbbing, I climbed back into the cave. Trick or not, I was going to look around while I was there. I picked up a stick and pried away some loose rocks on the walls, but I only found scorpions or spiders.

I scraped at the rusty rocks to see if there was a message under the rust. I thought it would be cool if I could find another clue.

I spent about two hours prying and scraping rocks in the cave. But I came up with nothing.

When I turned to leave the cave, I saw movement out of the corner of my eye. The creek bed was in the middle of nowhere, and I hadn't expected to see another person. Whatever caught my eye was purple-striped. That's not a color pattern you see in nature very often.

I put it out of my mind and limped home. I had to travel slowly. My ankle hurt a lot.

I hadn't found anything, but I had been hit by something. I had treasure fever big time. I was going to find that pirate loot, no matter what.

Chapter 4

SHAKE MY HAND

Big Fist finally noticed me the next week. He saw me sitting in the Local History room, looking at the book. I was hoping I'd be invisible in there. But I guess with the light on, it's more like being in a fish tank. Anyway, he burst into the room.

"What's up, Levi Loser?" he asked. He startled me, and I just about jumped out of my skin.

I was deep into the book. I looked up and glared at Big Fist.

Then I remembered that glaring at Big Fist can cause his fist to be planted in your face. I looked back down and shook my head.

"I said, what's up?" he repeated.

I knew there wouldn't be a chance of him getting bored and leaving me alone. I said flatly, "Local history. Got to write a report."

Big Fist folded his arms and leaned against the bookcase. He shook his head and stared at me. "Let's see," he said. He lunged toward me and grabbed the book.

"Looks pretty boring," he said. Then he tossed it back at me. "What class is your report for?" he asked.

"Um, it's extra credit," I said. "I'm doing it for social studies. I'm trying to bring up my grade."

"You're lying," he said.

"No, I'm not," I said. I really hated to disagree with him. In fact, I was lying. But I wasn't going to tell him about the treasure.

"So where's the report?" he asked.

"I'm just beginning," I said.

"You've been spending a lot of time in this room for just beginning a report," he said.

Rats, I thought. I said, "Well, it took me a while to figure out what to write about."

"So what are you writing about?" he asked, glaring at me.

I was blank. I couldn't think of anything to lie about.

"Shrimping," I blurted. "I'm writing about the shrimping industry."

Big Fist looked me over. His eyes narrowed.

"You're still lying," he said.

Then he walked out. I noticed he was wearing a shirt with purple stripes. It looked a lot like the flash of color I had seen at the cave last week. I remembered that he had other shirts like that, too.

I stared after Big Fist. No, I thought. He wouldn't have followed me. I knew he couldn't have been at the cave. There is no way he could have passed up the perfect place to beat me up.

I e-mailed Dad and told him I didn't find the treasure. I asked what the part in the song about the handshake meant.

In his message back Dad suggested an old oak tree in the same area, near the marsh. He said I'd understand why the tree was a clue when I saw it. Dad also said it was hard to describe the handshake in writing. He said to have Mom show me.

That night, Mom showed me how to shake and "twist just so" like the song said.

You start at the other person's elbow. Then you give a twist as you move your hand down the other person's arm toward the hand. By the time you get to the hand, you've twisted the arm around. If you twist right, the other person ends up with his arm twisted behind his back.

Right away on the first try, Mom had me in a hammerlock.

"How did you do that?" I asked her.

"Just keep twisting and don't let go of the other person," she said. "It gets to be a game. It's easy when the other person isn't doing it too. But it's hard when you're both trying. It's like a wrestling move."

We tried it again. This time Mom ended up with her arm behind her back.

"See, you've got it," she said, laughing.

"Were you just being nice, or do I really have it?" I asked.

We tried the handshake three more times. Each time Mom ended up in a hammerlock.

"You've got it," she said. "I'm not just being nice here. You are stronger and quicker than I am. I give up. You win."

I know it's not a big deal to beat your mom at something, but it felt pretty good to me.

Chapter 5

The next Saturday I found the tree.

At first I didn't see what Dad meant about it being a clue. It was really old. It was huge. It had a big, thick trunk and big, old branches that hung down to the ground.

Most of the oak trees around here look pretty windblown. They all lean away from the sea. They look like, if they could just pick up their roots, they'd move to higher ground.

I walked around the tree.

Suddenly I saw what Dad meant. The biggest branch twisted around the tree. It looked like the tree was giving itself a hug. Or maybe the tree just lost the handshake.

I figured it must have been a young tree a couple hundred years ago. Maybe the first Levi trained the branch to grow that way as a clue. Then he taught the song to his son.

It seemed strange, though, that no one had found the treasure.

I climbed around the tree. I looked at all the branches. I especially examined the one that was hugging the tree. The bark was the color of rust. I squatted down and looked at the roots. I wished I had brought a shovel.

I decided to come back later with one. I climbed the tree to have one more look. I thought maybe I could see a clue if I was actually in the tree.

I was hunting for something rusty. What I found was orange, a large shirt with orange stripes. It was moving down below me.

"Now what's up, Levi Loser? Looking for treasure?" Big Fist yelled up.

He must have gone back and looked at the book in the library. He must know about the buried treasure.

I thought about ignoring him. Maybe he'd just go away. But we were in the middle of nowhere. There was nobody to stop him from beating me up.

I decided to stay in the tree until he was gone. Maybe he was afraid of heights. Maybe I could climb better.

I was half his weight. For once being smaller seemed to be an advantage for me.

"What treasure?" I asked. "I'm just climbing a tree."

"I know about the treasure, Loser," Big Fist said. "And it's just as much mine as it is yours. I'm going to find it. Not you."

"Don't know what you're talking about," I yelled back.

I had climbed out on a branch, trying to get lost in the leaves. The next thing I heard was a loud crack. And the next thing I knew, I was lying on my back on the ground.

I lay blinking up at the sky through the tree. Slowly my head cleared. I must have knocked myself out for a few minutes.

I moved around a little. Nothing hurt. My head didn't even ache. Maybe I just had the wind knocked out of me.

Part of the broken branch lay next to me. Big Fist was standing over me, looking down.

"You okay?" he asked.

I moved my head from side to side. I sat up, then lay back down.

"Yeah, I'm okay," I said.

Big Fist walked away without another word. I lay still for a while longer, just thinking. Big Fist didn't come back. What if I had passed out again? What if my arm was broken? Thanks for the help, cousin.

Talk about your losers, I thought. Losers don't get much bigger than Big Fist.

I sang part of the song to myself again.

The treasure will grow,

generations will see,

And pits will rise to the sky.

I wondered what pits would rise to the sky. A pit is a hole. How can a hole rise? I got up and walked along the dry creek. I walked inland, past the cave.

 38

The pirate wouldn't have included that line in the poem for no reason.

It had to be a clue. It had to be.

I looked at the old trees growing along the creek. The trees in the old orchard were half dead. Wild grapevines were strangling many of them.

I didn't see any holes that were rising to the sky. I followed the creek bed back toward the bay.

As I rounded the last bend in the creek bed, I saw a big pile of rocks beside the marsh. I knew enough about rattlesnakes to stay away from the pile of rocks. Everybody who lives in rattlesnake territory knows that rattlers love rock piles.

I decided the rocks weren't there naturally. You just didn't see a big pile of rocks unless somebody had cleared a field.

Whoever had planted the orchard must have piled the rocks here.

In the past, farmers piled rocks around the edges of their land. The rock walls didn't go high enough to actually keep anybody out. They were used more to show boundaries.

I wondered why this farmer hadn't made a wall with the rocks instead of heaping them into this pile.

Then I remembered that Levi the First had been a farmer.

What if Levi One had cleared this land? He might have planted that orchard. He might have made that rock pile.

From a distance, I checked out the rock pile. I didn't see any rattlers. I knew that they sleep during the day.

But I wasn't going to take any chances.

From where I stood I could see that some of the big rocks had pits in them.

And pits will rise to the sky.

Levi the First had stacked those pitted rocks there on purpose, I thought. And underneath them, protected by rattlesnakes for two centuries, was his treasure.

Chapter 6

I went straight to the library on Saturday morning. I had to e-mail Dad right away.

I spent all of Sunday thinking of different ways I could move those rocks without upsetting any rattlers. There must have been a hundred big rocks. Some of them were huge. I knew I wouldn't be able to do it on my own.

On Monday, I got an e-mail from Dad.

Hey Kid,

So what happened with the tree? You didn't even mention it. Did you notice that one branch was bent backward? What can that mean?

Stay away from the pile of rocks. You know it's full of rattlers. I had forgotten about those rocks. Remember me telling you about the time I got bit? I was climbing on that pile of rocks. I was looking for the treasure.

I don't want something bad to happen to you, too. So please, stay away.

Besides, your mom doesn't need you in the hospital right now with a rattler bite. So stay away from the rocks.

Got it?

Love, Dad

Here's the e-mail I sent back to Dad.

Hey, Dad,

I promise I won't get bit. Remember Mrs.
Ellis? The rattlesnake catcher who lives out
on Bay Street? I invited her to come with
me next Saturday. She's going to show me
how to catch rattlesnakes. She thinks more
young people need to learn how to do it. She
says it's a public service to show me how to
do it. I know she won't let me get bit.

Oh, the tree. Did you ever notice the
branch that seems to be hugging the tree is
pointing straight to the pile of rocks?

Don't worry, Dad. I'll be fine.

I'm not telling Mom. That way she won't
have to worry.

Love, L.

I got another e-mail from Dad. It said:

L,

I still don't think you should go. But
it sounds like you're using your head
by having Mrs. Ellis go along. She knows
her way around snakes. I don't want your
mother to know about this. And I'd rather
you didn't learn to be a rattlesnake
catcher. They always end up getting bit. But
who am I to talk? Here I am in the Marines,
and in Iraq for the third time. I guess the
apple doesn't fall far from the tree.

Be careful.

Love, Dad

So, I had Dad's blessing, sort of. And Mom
thought I was safely roaming the marsh.

I knew most snakes were active at night.
I wouldn't be there at night. I even decided
that the part in the song about the sun
shining had to do with the snakes.

I was sure I had it figured out.

As I left on Saturday morning, Mom looked up from her newspaper.

"I see you have your long pants and hiking boots on," she said.

"Of course, Mom," I said.

"Okay, then have a good time, sweetie," she said.

This time I remembered to take a shovel. You could say I was being quite positive about getting to the bottom of that rock pile.

I worried a little about riding my bike through town carrying a shovel. At least it had a short handle.

I stuffed it into a green canvas duffel bag. The bag hid the shovel pretty well. It could have been anything in there. I tied it across the handlebars.

When I got to the marsh, Mrs. Ellis was waiting for me.

She was carrying a weird stick with long handles and a forked end. It looked like the kind of stick that's good for cooking hot dogs over a campfire.

She also had a white mesh bag. It looked like the kind of bag college kids bring dirty laundry home in, except her bag had a wide wire mouth with a drawstring.

I guess if you catch a snake, you want to be sure you can easily get it into the bag. Then you want to be sure you can close the bag quickly.

"Hi, Mrs. Ellis," I said. I smiled and held out my hand to shake.

She didn't smile, but she shook hands. "Are you afraid of snakes?" she asked.

"Kind of," I said.

"Good answer," Mrs. Ellis replied. "If you said you weren't afraid of snakes, I couldn't teach you to catch them. You have to fear and respect those creatures to be able to work with them."

I smiled.

"And if you said you were very afraid of snakes, I couldn't teach you, either," she went on. "You have to have the right amount of fear. If you're too afraid, the snake can sense that. Snakes are smart."

I didn't know if I agreed with her that snakes are smart. But I did know that snakes are quick. I respected that. I also knew that snakes won't bother you unless you bother them.

Since I was planning on destroying their home, I figured I'd better learn how to deal with them.

"I respect snakes," I said.

I hoped that was enough to convince her to teach me to catch them. I really didn't mean any harm to the snakes.

I just wanted what they were guarding.

"Catch!" Mrs. Ellis threw me the stick she was holding. I caught it.

"Good," she said. "You've got to be quick, too. You passed that test!"

I wondered how many more tests Mrs. Ellis would give me before she showed me how to catch a snake.

We began walking toward the marsh. She said, "When we get there, I'm going to show you how to avoid a snake. That's often the best way to deal with them."

"But," I said, "I want to move the rocks they live under."

Mrs. Ellis stopped in her tracks. She looked at me hard. "You what?" she asked.

"I want to move the rocks," I said.

"I heard you," she said. "I thought you said you respected snakes. I teach people to catch them if the snakes are in their way. It's another matter to go in there and destroy their home."

I shrugged my shoulders.

"Why would you want to do that, young man?" she asked.

I wasn't about to tell Mrs. Ellis that I was in search of buried pirate treasure.

For one thing, I didn't want her to think I was crazy. But mostly I didn't want her telling the whole town that there was pirate treasure under the pile of rocks.

So I lied.

"I have always wanted to climb these rocks," I said. "And my mom told me there are rattlers under them. So I thought I'd better know how to deal with them."

"Well, you don't have to move the rocks to climb on them," Mrs. Ellis said.

"Right," I said. "Actually, we need a couple of the rocks at home. Mom wants to put them in the garden. We don't need all the rocks. Just a couple."

Mrs. Ellis stared at me hard. I could almost see the wheels turning in her head. Was I lying? Was I being truthful? She must have decided that I was being honest because she continued to walk toward the rock pile.

"You can find rocks closer to home than these," she muttered. "I don't know why you need these rocks. You'll have to lug them clear across town."

"We like the pitted look," I explained. "Anyway, I'm not moving the rocks today," I told her. "I'll bring back a wheelbarrow later. Mom will bring the car. We'll put them in the trunk. I just want to be prepared. You know, just in case a snake attacks. Mom worries. You know how moms are."

Mrs. Ellis nodded. I had convinced her.

"If you move slowly and carefully, you won't have a problem," Mrs. Ellis said. "A snake will back off unless it's cornered. You can even move a rock. If the snake knows something is going to happen, the snake will leave. Just give it a warning. Give it time to get out of your way."

Mrs. Ellis stomped up to the rock pile. I could feel the ground shake under her boots. "Let them know you're coming," she said. I followed in her footsteps as she climbed onto the rock pile.

She spoke loudly. "So, do you see any rocks your mom likes?"

When we got to the top of the pile, I pointed to the topmost, largest, pitted rock. "Yes, ma'am. I bet Mom would like that one," I said. "It has some nice pits. Do you think any snakes would be disturbed if I pushed it off the pile?"

Mrs. Ellis peered closely in all the cracks around the rock. "I don't see any snakes up here. And they know we're up here. So if they leave, they'll go a different way," she explained. "I think it's safe. Try pushing it off. I'll watch out for you."

I bent down and put my shoulder against the rock. It was fairly round. I hoped it would roll down the pile once it got a start. I heaved with all my might.

It moved about an inch.

"Brace yourself and push with your foot," Mrs. Ellis said. "You have more strength in your leg than your arm."

I put my left foot against another, bigger rock and pushed with my right. The rock budged a little. Then it teetered on the edge of the pile.

The next thing I knew, it began to topple over. With a huge noise it rolled down the pile, bumping all the way down. I saw a couple of snakes race out. The noise must have been really loud inside the rock pile. Then I heard a scream.

I turned around and looked behind us. A green shirt was lying on the ground. Big Fist was inside it. He had been hiding in some weeds at the bottom of the pile, spying on us. His green shirt had mixed in with the weeds pretty well.

McLean County Unit #5
201-EJHS

Unfortunately, he hadn't been able to hear what Mrs. Ellis had said about making noise. He had been trying to be quiet so we wouldn't hear him. The snakes hadn't heard him either. He had been in the path of a fleeing rattler, and got bit on the arm.

Mrs. Ellis and I both saw the rattler slithering away.

Mrs. Ellis raced down the rock pile. First she made sure no more snakes were around. Then she told Big Fist to lie back and be quiet. She lightly tied a strip of cloth on each side of Big Fist's bite. Then she took out her cell phone and called 911.

"I'm going out to the road to wait for the ambulance," she told me. "You stay here with this young man. Keep him lying down. Keep him calm. Keep his arm low." Then she ran down the beach toward the road, about half a mile away.

Big Fist was lying on his back. I didn't have to do anything, because he had heard the instructions. He didn't move. His eyes were shut, but tears were running down the sides of his face and pooling in his ears.

I felt sorry that a rattler had bitten him. But I was really mad that he'd been spying on me. If I hadn't felt so sorry for him, I might have punched him in the face right then. He deserved it.

Chapter 7

DUST AND RUST

The ambulance came. The paramedics put Big Fist on a stretcher, loaded him into the ambulance, and raced off to the hospital. It seemed like it took forever for them to come and get him. In reality, he was gone in about fifteen minutes. Mrs. Ellis went with him.

I was glad I didn't have to go to the hospital. I didn't want to explain to Big Fist's parents what had happened. I wasn't sure what Mrs. Ellis would say, since she didn't know why he was there.

Did she notice that he was spying on us? Or did she think he was just a quiet kid? A weird, quiet kid.

I knew my mom would find out. Our town is too small for a kid to get a snakebite without everyone knowing about it.

I figured I'd explain everything to her when I got home.

On second thought, I decided not to. Maybe Big Fist wouldn't talk. Maybe Mrs. Ellis would forget my name. After all, I look a lot like about half the kids in this town. Why bring trouble to myself if I could avoid it? I decided to wait and see what Mom found out through the town grapevine.

I looked at the rock that had rolled off the pile. That was one rock down. There were about a hundred more to go to uncover the treasure.

I backed off and studied the rocks from a distance. I wasn't too crazy about going near them again. Although, I thought, all the snakes were probably gone now. I'd heard stories of people being out by themselves and getting snakebites. With nobody to get help, I could die all alone out here.

I decided to forget about moving more rocks that day.

I went back toward the beach and walked along it. Maybe the pile of rocks wasn't the right place after all. Maybe that crafty old pirate had set up a bunch of clues just to play tricks on people. Maybe it was just a song, and there was no buried treasure. Old Levi the First was getting a good chuckle, wherever he was.

Saturday night, Dad called. He talked to Mom for so long I was afraid I wouldn't get a chance to talk.

Finally, I got to talk to him. I told him I didn't get far with the day's project. I had to be careful what I said, because I knew Mom was listening.

"You know there are lots of clues in the song," Dad said.

"Any more from you?" I asked.

"You're on your own now," he said. "I've told you what I remember. There are enough clues to keep you busy for months," he added. "But you're the seventh generation to hunt for the treasure. Nobody's found it. Who knows if it's really out there?"

After we hung up, I thought about what Dad had said. I didn't want to quit searching, but I was out of ideas.

By Sunday Mom had heard about Big Fist's snakebite. Luckily, my name hadn't popped up in the story.

I seemed to be off the hook. Big Fist wasn't going to admit that he was spying on me. And Mrs. Ellis forgot my name.

I strapped the duffel bag to my bike and went back out searching. After all, Big Fist was still in the hospital in Rockport, so I knew he wasn't following me.

I walked past the shrimpers' docks and down to the beach with my shovel. I sang the song to myself. I thought about the last part.

Be mindful to scrape the rust.

Take care that the sun shines on it too,

So the gold doesn't turn to dust.

I thought about what could rust. Glass can't rust. But just about anything metal near the ocean can. Something that was buried two hundred years ago might be a big pile of rust now.

The old book said that Levi the First had died in 1870. So if he buried his treasure toward the end of his life, it might only be about 150 years old. Could gold rust? The old pirate had said the treasure was gold.

I thought about the clue about the sun shining. If the sun didn't shine on it, it might turn to dust. What turns to dust? I figured, in time, just about everything turns to dust.

I put the shovel away and headed home. I decided I needed to finish reading the old library book. Maybe there were more clues I hadn't found yet.

Chapter 8

I was safe for the next week. Big Fist didn't come back to school. I figured when he did show up, he'd really want to punch me out for seeing him cry.

I had a lot of homework that week, so I didn't get to read more of the old history book until Friday. On Friday, though, I stayed at the library until I'd finished it.

I had cleared it with Mom ahead of time. I would leave for home at eight, when the library closed.

I can't say I found any clues in the old book. But I learned more things about the old pirate.

People in the book said that Levi the Second wasn't proud of his dad's past. He thought being a pirate was no way to make a living. Pirates do bad things. They steal. Maybe they even kill. Anyway, when Levi the Second got old enough to understand where his dad's money had come from, he was ashamed.

Levi the Second married when he was quite young. He wanted to move away, but he didn't have a trade, besides shrimping. And you can't be a shrimper if you don't live by the water.

He and his wife had one child, Levi the Third. Levi Two went off to fight in the Civil War. He left his wife and son here in Texas.

His plan was to return and take them north to live after the war.

He didn't join the Rebel Army. He went up north to join the Union Army. He fought to free the slaves. Levi the Second was killed during the Civil War. That left his dad to help raise Levi the Third.

Levi the Third was born in 1850. And Levi the First died in 1870. So Levi the pirate had twenty years to teach the song to his grandson. If his son, Levi the Second, didn't want to have anything to do with him, maybe Levi the First made up the song especially for his grandson.

That made sense to me. Maybe Levi the First didn't want Levi the Second to have his fortune. Maybe, because Levi the Second was ashamed of the fortune, Levi the First hid it from him.

I guess Levi the Third didn't get the clues, though. There isn't a record of him finding the treasure.

Levi the Third was a shrimper. He and all the Levis after him stayed in this area. I wrote Dad and told him what I thought had happened. He wrote back:

L,

You're right. All the Levis were shrimpers, until me. The service, or military, has been a big part of almost every Levi's life, too. Not just Levi the Second.

Even Levi the First might have fought with Lafitte in the War of 1812. I think the service is why the family has always hung around here. The men go off and fight in wars. They leave their wives and children with the rest of the family. After they get out of the service, they want to come home and live their normal lives.

That's what I want to do after Iraq.

Your grandpa was in Vietnam.

 68

Your great-grandpa was in World War II. I think a Levi was in World War I, too.

That's a good theory about how the song got started. You just might be right.

Love, Dad

I guess, since I'm a Levi, I have the service to look forward to. Maybe there won't be any more wars when I'm older. I'll just join the service to see the world.

Actually, Dad told me that's what he had planned when he joined the service. He was going to get a little free travel. Then he'd come back home and go shrimping every morning. If he didn't sell his day's catch, we'd eat it for dinner. There are worse things than having to eat shrimp every day.

He said Grandpa had planned the same thing. But wars have a way of sneaking up on you and changing your life.

Take Levi the Second, for example.

Anyway, I didn't find any more clues about the treasure. I knew the rock pile had to be the place. So I went back to ask Mrs. Ellis if she would still teach me to catch snakes. She said Big Fist getting bitten had changed her mind. She wasn't worried for her own safety, but she wouldn't be responsible for any more kids getting snakebites.

"I won't get bitten," I said.

"No," she said.

"I'm too smart to get bitten," I said.

"What part of no don't you understand?" she yelled at me.

"But!"

Her screen door slammed in my face. As she went inside, she yelled over her shoulder, "And stay away from that rock pile!"

I sat down on Mrs. Ellis's front porch steps. I crossed my arms on my knees and laid my head on my arms. I didn't know anyone else who could teach me to catch snakes. Mrs. Ellis was the only expert around.

I thought about all the Levis. About how they were all shrimpers. Then I remembered Grandpa's old shrimp boat. Could it have been the original shrimp boat Levi the First had used? Could the treasure be on the boat?

My heart sank. What if the treasure was the boat that Levi the First had bought? Maybe he put all his money into a boat. Some hurricane probably took care of that shrimp boat a long time ago.

I walked home, still confused. Was there a treasure or wasn't there?

Chapter 9

The next afternoon I was playing a video game when I heard a knock at the door. Big Fist was standing there. Next to him stood his mother, who was holding something out to me.

"Levi, we just had to come and thank you for saving Billie's life!" she said. She thrust a pie into my hands.

My mom came out from the kitchen.

"Hello, Arlene. What a surprise. Please, come in," Mom said.

I had planned to grab the pie and slam the door. Now Mom was asking if Arlene would like a cup of coffee. "Billie" made himself comfortable on our couch.

"To what do we owe this nice surprise?" Mom asked as I stood there holding the pie.

"Well, we had to thank Levi for saving Billie's life!" Arlene said.

Mom looked surprised, but she covered it well. Then she looked at me. I grinned. I had no idea how this conversation would turn out. About all I could do was wait and see what happened next.

"So," Mom said. "Big, er, Billie, are you feeling okay now?"

Arlene beamed at Billie and nodded.

"Yes, ma'am," said Big Fist. He nodded too, but he didn't add any details.

Everyone was quiet for a moment. I'm sure Mom was trying to think how to word a question to make it sound like she knew what was going on. I wasn't about to leap in with anything. Big Fist looked embarrassed.

Finally, Arlene spoke. "I got the peaches for that pie from the old orchard by the bay. I just canned them in July!"

"Well, it looks delicious," Mom said. "Shall we all have a piece?"

"I'll help you," I offered.

"No, you stay here, Levi," Mom said. "Entertain our guests."

I didn't know how to entertain guests. I couldn't sing or dance. I couldn't even tell a joke. So I just sat there and stared at the wall above their heads.

Arlene cleared her throat. "I really don't know how we can ever thank you, Levi. Mrs. Ellis told me how you stayed with Billie and made him comfortable while she went to get some help."

Her voice caught. She was dabbing at her eyes. Big Fist was the color of boiled beets.

She went on. "I'm so glad you boys have become friends. I'm glad Billie has someone to do things with on the weekends now. I suppose spending time at the library has drawn you two close. I just knew that would be a good thing for Billie."

I began to shake my head. I had to set things straight. But Mom came back into the room with a tray of pie and coffee.

"Here you go," she said as she passed out plates and cups. "This pie looks great. Why, I haven't been out to that orchard in years."

Arlene said, "I tried to think of what I could do to thank Levi. I suggested that Billie invite him for supper, but Billie is a little shy."

Shy, my eye, I thought, trying not to smile. He's downright antisocial.

"Anyway," she continued, "I decided that since the orchard is near where Billie got the snakebite, maybe a nice pie would express our thankfulness."

Mom looked at me.

"Well, it's really good," I said. Then out of the blue, I asked, "Who does that orchard belong to, anyway?"

"Levi!" Mom said. She must have thought I was trying to say that I thought the peaches were stolen.

We finished our pie and Arlene thanked me again.

Big Fist didn't have much to say. But he did show us his bite. It had swollen quite a lot by the time the ambulance had come. Now all you could see were two faint marks with a little purplish bruise around them.

After they left, Mom stood in front of me. "What really happened?" she asked.

"A snake came out of a pile of rocks and bit him," I said.

"Where were you?" she asked.

"On top of the pile of rocks," I said.

"How does Mrs. Ellis fit into all this?" she asked. "I knew she was with Billie when he got bit. But no one told me you were there. Including you."

"Guess I forgot," I said. I looked down.

"You don't forget something like that, Levi. What was going on?" she asked.

"Mrs. Ellis was helping me move a rock. Big Fist was in the way. We didn't know he was there. And neither did the snake, until it was too late," I explained.

Mom just glared at me. "I don't suppose I'll ever know the full story, will I?" she asked.

I smiled. "Really, Mom, it was nothing."

"I'll bet," she said. "Well, you can help me take this tray back into the kitchen."

I stared down at the tray. Bits of golden crust and peach juice stained the plates. Suddenly, the old treasure song became clear. I knew what it all meant!

Chapter 10

Dear Dad,

It's the peach trees, isn't it? It's got to be the peaches. Peaches have pits. Peaches need sun. You taste peaches. Some of the peach trees are all twisty, like that live oak tree.

Those trees in that old orchard were Levi's fortune. Then he wrote that poem to confuse us all.

I did an Internet search on the orchard. It was his property a long time ago.

I couldn't tell how he got it. He might have just kind of claimed it. Or maybe he bought it. Anyway, it belongs to either the county now or some family member who wants to pay off years and years of property taxes. Am I right?

Love, Levi

Dear Levi,

You guessed it. That's exactly what I came up with. But I never knew for sure. I didn't have the Internet to help me. I just asked my dad. He said he'd come up with the same thing. So had his dad, and on down the line.

You probably know more about it than the rest of us.

So, welcome to the Levi Viggers Peach Pit Club!

That old orchard is the family treasure. And that's why we all end up in the Army, the Navy, or now the Marines. Got to earn a living because you can't live on peaches, my boy.

Have you thought about what you want to do when you grow up? Do you prefer any branch of the service? The country really will probably stop having wars one of these days.

Sorry if the peaches disappoint you.

Love, Dad

Dear Dad,

I am disappointed. Are you sure the treasure isn't buried somewhere inside the orchard?

There's nothing wrong with the service, but I'd kind of like to go to college.

I really like looking up stuff on the Internet. It might be interesting to find some kind of job where I can do a lot of that. Or maybe that's what you do in college.

Keep safe,

L.

_____

Dear Son,

Don't bother to dig in the orchard. Between your grandpa and me, that orchard has been dug. And who knows how many times it was dug up before we were born. With all that digging, it's a miracle that the peach trees are still alive. The peaches are the treasure. College sounds fine. We'll start saving. Keep digging on the Internet. You're finding some interesting treasures there, too.

Love, Dad

So we decided that the pirate's treasure was peaches. I really thought that was the pits. I felt like the old pirate was still playing jokes on everyone, a hundred and fifty years after he died.

I had another, bigger disappointment. Big Fist wouldn't leave me alone. At first he tried bossing me around. Then, when I acted like I didn't care, he did a switch on me. He didn't want to beat me up anymore.

Big Fist seemed to think he owed me his life. Actually he owed it to Mrs. Ellis. And I even tried to point that out. But it didn't seem to matter. Big Fist had chosen me as his buddy, and he wasn't used to being told no.

I figured he was just waiting until I started looking for the treasure again so he could spy on me. So I told him about the peaches. I thought that would get him off my back.

All he said was, "That can't be it."

I liked his attitude. And I agreed with him.

One day at the library he and I had an argument about the treasure. If we found it, who would it belong to? He said, "You know, I have as much right to the treasure as you do. I'm a Viggers, too."

I said, "So help yourself to all the peaches you want."

"That's not what I mean," he said. "If there really was a treasure, I'd have as much right to it as you do. Levi the First was my great, great, great, great, great grandfather too, you know."

"No, he was your great uncle," I said.

"No, he was my grandfather," he said. "My dad is your dad's cousin. That means my grandfather was your grandfather's brother, right?" he said.

I thought about it. "Yeah," I said.

"So," he said, "that means my great grandfather was your great grandfather too. He was Levi Viggers the Fifth. Besides, I know the song too. I've been looking for that treasure a lot longer than you have."

I had to admit he was right. He had as much claim to the pirate as I did. I always thought because my name was Levi that I was the special kid.

But there were probably hundreds of people who could claim the treasure. Finders, keepers. That was the rule. I'd just have to be the one to find that treasure.

With the library time and all, Big Fist was spending quite a lot of time with me. I realized after a while that he really wasn't so bad. Once you got past the fist.

Chapter 11

Something good came from spending time at the library. My grades went up. Way up. I was getting organized. I'd get my homework done first thing after school. Then I'd read a book or e-mail Dad. I was feeling pretty good about myself.

Months went by. I put the treasure on the back burner. Mom needed me around to do holiday stuff. It was January when I started thinking about treasure again.

I kept wondering why that pile of rocks was there. When you think about it, it's a lot of work to make a pile of rocks. It's much easier to build a fence around an orchard.

So why would the pirate make a pile of rocks? The first Saturday in January, I put on layers of clothes, gloves, and a stocking cap. The whole works. I walked to the rock pile. I climbed on top and began chucking the smaller rocks. You're pretty safe from snakes in the winter. It's too cold for them. They can hardly move. Plus, if one should wake up and try to attack, I was well covered.

My problem was my ability. I guess I should call it my inability. I could only move a few of the smaller rocks.

I went home and actually phoned Big Fist. I asked him to help me.

"I don't think so," he said.

"Why not? The snakes are asleep," I said. "You can wear layers. You'll be safe."

"The treasure isn't there," he said. "Why even bother?"

I told him my theory about the pile of rocks. I reminded him that half of the treasure would be his. I had to get to the bottom of that pile of rocks. And Big Fist was the biggest, strongest guy I knew. Plus, he's family.

"Okay," he said. "I'll meet you there in half an hour."

He looked a little green in the face when I met him at the rock pile. "This will be good for you," I said.

"Yeah, like a punch in the face would be good for you," he said.

I'd almost forgotten how afraid of him I used to be. He started laughing.

"Just kidding," he said.

The joke made us both feel better. We stomped toward the rock pile in case any snakes were awake. Then we climbed up. We didn't see anything.

Once we got to the top, we worked together to roll rocks off the pile. After about two hours, we were both worn out. I was sweating like it was July. Chucking big rocks is really hard work.

"Too bad we have to go to the library every day after school," Big Fist said.

"Yeah, but it's almost dark after school anyway. We can get all our homework done during the week. Then we can meet here again Saturday morning," I said.

We came back the next Saturday, and every Saturday in January and February.

I had been wrong about the number of rocks on that pile. There were at least two hundred of them. Some of them wouldn't move at all.

On the first Saturday in March, Big Fist said, "I'm done. You can have the treasure."

He jumped off the rocks and started heading for home.

"Why?" I yelled after him. "We only have two more layers of rocks."

"Get an end loader," he yelled back. "See you at the library."

Chapter 12

On Monday, I tracked down Big Fist at the library. "You can't quit now," I said. "We're almost done. Just a couple more weeks."

Big Fist looked embarrassed. "I said I'm done!" he said.

I backed off. But I needed Big Fist's help. So, at 5:30, I was waiting outside the library. While I was waiting, I thought about last fall. I had been running out the door to avoid Big Fist because I was afraid of him. Now he was the one who seemed afraid.

Big Fist came out the door. For a brief moment, he looked like the old Big Fist. His face was shut. He walked past me.

I caught up with him. "It's the snakes, isn't it?" I said.

"Yeah, it's the snakes," he said. "I can still see that sucker coming straight at me, his mouth wide open, his fangs out. It happened before I could blink."

"You know it happened that way because of where you were," I said.

"And we're almost to the ground," he said. "You know there are snakes in that pile. We're getting closer to them."

"I don't think there are snakes in there anymore," I said. "I think all the noise we've been making ran them out."

"Oh, there are snakes all right," he said.

"So, we're prepared this time," I said.

"No," Big Fist said. "It's getting too warm. We can't keep wearing tons of layers. We'll melt." He punched the air.

"And besides," he said, "it's getting warm enough for the snakes to be moving around. I read that on the Internet. Rattlers are the most active in the spring."

He had a point there. "Okay," I said. "I'll do it myself."

Big Fist stopped walking. He looked at me. "It's not worth it," he said. "And you can't do it yourself. You're not strong enough. Besides, you can't go there by yourself. If you do get bit, you need somebody to get help."

"I'll be there on Saturday, whether you are or not," I said.

So Saturday morning I was out on the much lower mound of rocks.

I was pushing with my feet. I was sitting on rocks and using my back to push. But I couldn't get any rocks to budge. By pushing them off the heap, we'd created a wider, lower pile. Now there was nowhere for the rocks to fall. Someone had to pick them up to move them.

I was standing on the rocks wondering how much it would cost to rent an end loader when I was hit in the back of the head. It felt like a bird had flown into me. I turned around. Big Fist was standing there with his mittens in his hands. Beside him were two shovels and a giant crowbar.

"Leverage," he said. I smiled.

With the crowbar, the shovels, and lots of sweat, we got the big rocks out of the middle of the pile. We had taken a mound shape and made it into a donut shape. And we didn't see a single rattlesnake.

We dug inside the donut hole. Our theory was that the old pirate would have buried his treasure smack dab in the middle of the mound, not to one side. Just in case, though, we threw the shovels of dirt as far as we could. We might have to move more rocks, but we didn't want to shovel twice.

About a foot down, my shovel scraped something. I hoped it wasn't another rock. We uncovered a square shape and used the crowbar to pry up a wooden and metal box.

Big Fist and I looked at each other.

I can only imagine what I looked like. But Big Fist's eyes were about to pop right out of his head.

The box wouldn't open. We thought we should be gentle with it, so we didn't try the huge crowbar. We brought the box back to my house.

Mom didn't know how to open the box either. We called the fire department. They suggested that we call the maritime museum in Rockport. So we did.

We ended up taking the box down to Rockport where a woman opened it with a screwdriver. We could have done that.

Anyway, inside we found the real pirate's treasure. It included a dagger with jewels in the handle. There were several gold coins, some gold beads, and a gold box with a tree on the front. It looked a lot like the big old oak tree because it bent to one side. The lady said the box was a snuffbox, whatever that is.

There was also a pendant in the shape of a salamander with rubies on it. These pieces were all wrapped up in moldy cloth. There was also a thick piece of folded paper. When we touched it, it fell apart.

Mom had brought the camera, so we took pictures of everything. The lady said she was going to have the paper analyzed. She was also going to call some big museum in Washington DC.

* * *

Now we just have to figure out who gets what. We think the land belongs to the county, but the family might get to keep it. I don't care. I'm just glad we found the loot.

A photographer from the Rockport paper came out and took a picture of Big Fist and me on the rock pile with our shovels. We both have big smiles on our faces.

The headline says, "Local Cousins Find Pirate Treasure."

We e-mailed the picture and article to Dad. This is what he sent back:

L,

Congratulations! You are the Levi who found the loot.

Wouldn't old Levi the First be surprised to know how long his treasure was buried?

Your search and your library time have sure made my tour in Iraq go faster. I'll see you in a month!

Love, Dad

Big Fist and I are already planning what we'll do with all the money we'll get. First we'll go to college. Then we'll open a detective agency and specialize in lost treasures. I want to call it "Brains and Big Fist." He wants to call it "Big Fist and Brains."

I think we'll flip an old gold coin over it.

More About the Pirate Jean Lafitte

Jean Lafitte (ZHON lah-FEET) was famous in the early part of the nineteenth century for being a cruel, violent pirate, and a charming, friendly man. Lafitte lived and worked in Barataria Bay, which is where the Mississippi meets the Gulf of Mexico, in Louisiana. Legend says that the famous pirate Blackbeard hid there from the British a hundred years earlier!

In those days, Lafitte worked as a privateer. His job was to take goods from enemy ships. Lafitte and his men, who also lived in Barataria, began their privateering careers by capturing Spanish and English ships for the French. By 1808, Lafitte and his brother, Pierre, were smuggling goods between Barataria and New Orleans.

Soon, the Lafittes became involved in a plot to attack Texas. The United States government stopped the attack and destroyed the Lafittes' land and property in Barataria.

During the War of 1812, the British asked Lafitte to help them capture New Orleans. Instead, Lafitte helped the United States. In return for his help, Lafitte hoped for a pardon from the U.S. for his actions against Texas. He received the pardon, but did not get his goods back from Barataria.

In 1816, Lafitte went to Galveston, Texas, as an agent for the Spanish secret service. Galveston Island became a center for smuggling and privateering. Jean Lafitte was called the Master of Galveston from 1817 until 1820. In 1820, he was driven from Galveston. It is believed that he went to Mexico until 1825. After 1825, there are no records of the pirate Jean Lafitte.

ABOUT THE AUTHOR

M. J. Cosson has written almost 40 books. She
lives with her husband, George, and two dogs,
Clancy and Clementine, and cat, Carrie Chapman
Catt. She has two sons and daughters-in-law
and three grandchildren. She loves all animals
(even poisonous ones) and shares her yard with
tarantulas, scorpions, rattlesnakes, and centipedes,
but she especially loves elephants.

ABOUT THE ILLUSTRATOR

Brann Garvey grew up in the great state of Iowa.
He graduated from the Minneapolis College of Art
and Design with a degree in illustration. Brann is
usually found with one or more of the following:
a pencil in his hand, a comic book, a remote for
watching DVDs, or his pet kitty, Iggy. When the
weather is nice, Brann likes to play disc golf, and
he proudly points out that Iowa is one of the
world's centers for the sport. Iggy does not play.

⟨⟨ GLOSSARY ⟩⟩

ashamed (uh-SHAYMD)—feeling embarrassed and guilty

boundary (BOUN-duh-ree)—the line that separates one area from another

debate (di-BATE)—a discussion between sides with different views

hammerlock (HAM-ur-lok)—a wrestling hold

leverage (LEV-ur-ij)—the power gained by using a lever to move something

oil refinery (OIL ri-FYE-nuh-ree)—a factory where oil is purified and made into products

pendant (PEN-duhnt)—a hanging ornament, often on a necklace

privateer (pry·vuh-TEER)—a sailor who has a license to attack enemy ships

rumor (ROO-mur)—something said by many people although it may not be true

theory (THEER-ee)—an idea based on some facts or evidence but not proved

ᗕᗢᗢ **DISCUSSION QUESTIONS** ᗢᗢᗒ

1. At the beginning of the story, Levi is afraid of Big Fist. By the end of the story, the two are good friends. Who do you think changed? Or was it both boys?

2. At the beginning of the story, Levi's grades are low. He spends his time playing video games or watching TV. How does Levi's daily behavior change by the time he's found the treasure? Why do you think these changes happened?

4. How would things have been different for Levi if he had never spent time in the library? Do you think he would have found out about Levi the First and the treasure? Do you think he would have spent as much time talking to his father?

⌒⌒ WRITING PROMPTS ⌒⌒

1. Can you think of a time when you had bad feelings about someone you didn't know well? Once you got to know the person, did your feelings change? Write about how you felt before you knew the person and then how you felt afterwards.

2. Think about how you would feel if you found out you were related to a pirate. Would it be a good thing or a bad thing? Write about how you would react to the news.

3. Write about the first thing you would do if you found a pirate's treasure. Would you buy something for yourself or for someone else? Would you save the money for something? Or would you donate it to a charity?

ALSO PUBLISHED BY STONE ARCH BOOKS

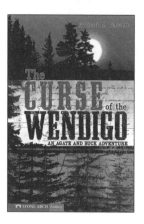

The Curse of the Wendigo
by Scott R. Welvaert

Agate and Buck set out on a spine-tingling adventure through the haunted Canadian woods in search of their missing parents. An ancient curse is set into motion, and soon they too are being hunted.

Rock Art Rebel
by M. J. Cosson

Beto's urban art is labeled graffiti by the police, so the boy is sent to spend the summer with faraway relatives. Then Beto discovers art in an unexpected place, and he's the only one who can save it.

The Ghost's Revenge
by M. Peschke

The ancient Comanche warrior that Zack sees in his dreams has begun to appear in real life. As the line between real life and Zack's dream world blurs, he embarks on a dangerous journey of terror and discovery.

Poison Plate
by M. Sobel Spirn

When Mark moves in with a family who owns a restaurant, he is wrongfully accused of whipping up a diabolically delicious dinner.

ᑕᖇᑎ **INTERNET SITES** ᑎᕼᑫ

Do you want to know more about subjects related to this book? Or are you interested in learning about other topics? Then check out FactHound, a fun, easy way to find Internet sites.

Our investigative staff has already sniffed out great sites for you!

Here's how to use FactHound:

1. Visit *www.facthound.com*

2. Select your grade level.

3. To learn more about subjects related to this book, type in the book's ISBN number: **1598890689**.

4. Click the **Fetch It** button.

FactHound will fetch the best Internet sites for you!